THE WORLD OF CHAOS

VESPICK THE WASP QUEEN

With special thanks to Cherith Baldry

For Max Wiltshire

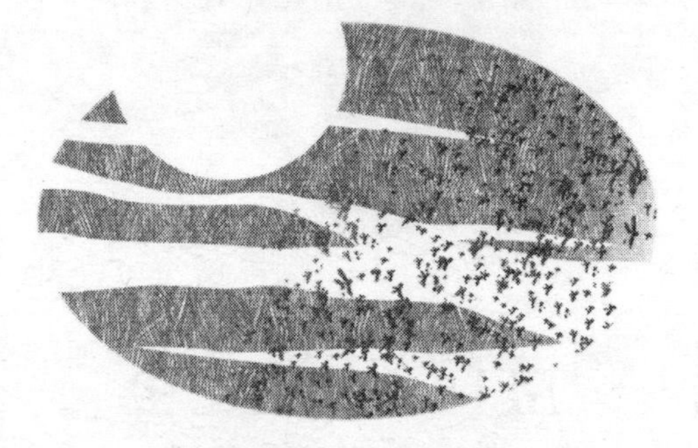

www.beastquest.co.uk

ORCHARD BOOKS
338 Euston Road, London NW1 3BH
Orchard Books Australia
Level 17/207 Kent St, Sydney, NSW 2000

A Paperback Original
First published in Great Britain in 2010

Beast Quest is a registered trademark of Beast Quest Limited
Series created by Beast Quest Limited, London

A CIP catalogue record for this book is available from
the British Library.

ISBN 978 1 40830 728 1

10

Printed and bound by CPI Group (UK) Ltd, Croydon, CR0 4YY

Orchard Books is a division of Hachette Children's Books,
an Hachette UK company

www.hachette.co.uk

Vespick the Wasp Queen

BY ADAM BLADE

THE ICY D
KAYONIAN MARSHLANDS
KAYONIAN PLAINS
KAYONIAN FOREST

ERT
Kayonia
THE GOLDEN VALLEY
MEATON

Hail, young warriors!

Tom has set out on a Quest of his own choosing, and I have the honour of helping with magic learnt from the greatest teacher of them all: my master, Aduro. Tom's challenges will be great: a new kingdom, a lost mother and six more Beasts under Velmal's spell. Tom isn't just fighting to save a kingdom. He's fighting to save those lives closest to him and to prove that love can conquer evil. Can it? Tom will only find out by staying strong and keeping the flame of hope alive. As long as no foul wind blows it out...

Yours truly,

The apprentice, Marc

PROLOGUE

Queen Romaine of Kayonia gazed angrily at a wasp that flew through the window of the north turret. She batted it to the floor and crushed it under her heel. The young wizard Marc was speaking to her, but she couldn't hear because of the buzzing in her ears.

"Speak up!" she said.

Marc moved closer to her. "Your Majesty, the plague of wasps is getting worse," he reported. "Your people are beginning to panic. Something must be done."

Letting out a sigh, the queen paced from one side of the turret room to the other. Her copper-coloured hair flicked out behind her and her knuckles were white from gripping her bone staff so tightly.

"The wasps have chased away the last of my palace guards," she said with a growl of frustration. "Those who haven't gone to deal with the rioters and looters. The kingdom has been plunged into utter chaos." She banged her staff on the floor. "I am a warrior queen, but against this threat I am helpless!"

"Your Majesty—" Marc began. He broke off as the sound of screams from below rose above the buzzing.

Queen Romaine rushed to the window of the tower, with the young wizard by her side. Leaning out, she gazed down into the city square.

The wasps had formed themselves into a swirling, writhing swarm. They danced above the ground, clustering around a shape that the queen couldn't make out clearly. Then she gasped in horror as the cloud of wasps divided into separate swarms.

Hovering above the square was a creature as tall as two large men. Four fluttering wings sprouted from its back. A human-shaped torso ended in a body striped in yellow and black. It tapered into a long, cruel sting that glowed brilliant green.

"She must be the queen wasp!" Romaine whispered.

She stifled a cry as she saw the smaller swarms of wasps swirling around her fleeing subjects, stinging them over and over again as the people tried vainly to beat off their attacks. "How can this be happening?" she demanded, her fists clenched around her bone staff.

"It is the work of the dark wizard, Velmal," Marc told her. "He has travelled around your kingdom, bringing unrest and destruction wherever he goes. That giant wasp, Vespick, is a Beast enslaved to Velmal. She has dared to set foot in your capital – and that means Velmal himself can't be far behind. He—"

"Look!" Queen Romaine interrupted, pointing down. Vespick had caught sight of her and was flying up towards the top of the turret, with the swarm following in her wake. The Beast soared past the window, glaring at Romaine with bulging eyes before vanishing from sight.

Romaine clutched at the windowsill as the stone tower shook and rattled. "She dares to batter the walls of my castle!" she shouted.

More wasps buzzed in through the turret window. They flew straight at Marc and Romaine. The Kayonian queen slapped her hand to her neck and let out another sharp cry as two of the wasps pierced her skin with their stings.

The wizard stretched out his hands and murmured a spell. A bubble of shimmering blue light formed around him and the queen, keeping the rest of the wasps at bay. The wasps buzzed angrily against it, only to bounce off again.

"What can I do to help my people when I'm trapped inside here?" the queen asked.

"There is only one person who can help any of us now," Marc replied gravely. "One saviour who can protect the whole of Kayonia from this evil wizard."

Queen Romaine reached up and caught a stray wasp that was trapped inside the magical bubble. Her hand closed tightly, ignoring the sting.

"This 'saviour' had better come quickly," she muttered.

CHAPTER ONE

THE FINAL BEAST

"Tom, are you hurt?" Elenna asked anxiously.

Tom sat on the ground at the edge of the forest, his head in his hands. He thought the searing pain would split it apart. But worse than the pain were the visions of his dying mother that the evil wizard Velmal had shown him. Tom wanted to forget them, but Freya's sickness remained vivid in his mind. He could still see her lying on a blood-red floor, as pale as death.

I can't *give up now,* he thought. *Not when I'm so close to finding the last ingredient for the potion that will save her.*

Silver's wet tongue swiped over Tom's face. He looked up to see Elenna and the grey wolf crouched beside him, both with worry in their eyes. Somewhere behind Tom, Storm let out an anxious whinny.

"I'm all right," Tom said hoarsely. He struggled to his feet, trying to ignore the quivering in his legs. He straightened his shoulders. "Velmal's dirty tricks aren't going to stop me completing the Quest," he vowed. "There's only one more Beast to go!"

"What does the amulet say, Tom?" Elenna asked eagerly.

Tom pulled out the magical Amulet of Avantia on its cord around his neck, and watched the map form on its rear surface. The trail it showed led to the south-east.

"Meaton..." Tom murmured, reading the letters that appeared across the region. "That's the place we have to make for."

"Look at that!" Elenna pointed to the tiny picture of a castle, with towers and battlements and a flag flying from the topmost turret. "Meaton must be the capital city, where the Warrior Queen Romaine lives. She... Oh!"

Tom gasped as he saw what had startled his friend. The image of a wasp flying around the turret had flickered into view. Its wings whirred angrily and it flourished an evil-looking sting that glowed a sickly green. The name 'Vespick' appeared beside it in fiery letters.

"That's the next Beast!" Tom exclaimed. "The whole of the city must be in danger."

"But where's the next ingredient for the potion?" Elenna asked, peering at the amulet. "The map has always shown it to us before. Without it we can't save your mother."

"I know," Tom replied grimly. "Maybe the Beast is carrying the ingredient, whatever it is. Well, there's only one way to find out."

He turned and marched firmly over to Storm. "We have some travelling to do," he said as he swung himself into the saddle and reached out a hand to pull Elenna up behind him.

And we've no idea when the night will

come, he added to himself. *Or how long my mother still has to live.*

"We'd better get going," he said.

After a short ride, Tom reined Storm to a stop at the edge of a cornfield. Ahead of him, the crop waved and rustled in the breeze.

"Careful, Silver!" Elenna warned her wolf. "Don't go running off."

Silver let out a whine and sat obediently beside the stallion.

"That's the way we have to go," Tom said, pulling out the amulet again to give their route a quick check. The road leading around the cornfield would take them a good distance out of their way. It would be much quicker to cut across it, straight towards nearby Meaton.

"It's a farmer's field," Elenna said uneasily. "We're bound to damage some of the crop."

"We can't afford to waste time," Tom said.

Pulling his father's compass from his pouch, he gazed down at the dial marked with *Destiny* and *Danger*, and watched until the whirling needle had stopped. It pointed to *Destiny*: straight across the cornfield. "That settles it," he said, thrusting the compass back into the pouch. "We have to go this way."

Tom guided Storm into the cornfield, careful not to crush more of the crops than he could help. Silver padded along behind, in the trail made by the stallion's hooves.

As they headed deeper into the field, Tom thought he heard a rustling behind him, though there was no breeze to stir the ears of corn.

He glanced over his shoulder, but saw nothing.

"Did you hear something?" he asked Elenna.

His friend shook her head. "Only the corn brushing against Storm."

Tom wasn't sure. *My head still aches,* he thought, gritting his teeth against the searing pain. *Maybe that's making me hear things*. He tried to stifle his anxiety, but it still pricked at him. "We have to push on," he said, half to himself. "There's a Beast waiting for us!"

Soon Tom could make out the line of a hedge at the far side of the cornfield, and beyond it, gentle hills covered with grass. "Storm will be able to have a real gallop there," he said, pointing forward. "With any luck we'll be in Meaton soon."

While he was speaking, the sky suddenly grew dark.

It can't be night so soon! Not even in Kayonia!

Storm reared onto his hind legs as a rope mesh was hurled over them, trapping them under its heavy folds.

A net! Tom thought.

Storm tossed his head, whinnying in panic, and Silver let out a long howl of protest.

Tom struggled to reach his sword to cut through the thick rope, but it was no use. They were trapped!

CHAPTER TWO

PRISONERS

As Tom tore furiously at the cords, men crowded around, securing the trap they had thrown. They seemed to have come from nowhere, but Tom guessed that they had been lurking in the corn. Peering through the thick strands of the net, he could see that their clothes were ragged and their hair was matted. Their grimy faces were angry and they were shouting as they waved spears and scythes.

"Thieves!"

"Trespassers!"

"We don't want you here!"

One of the men stepped forward and started to gather up the folds of the net. "We watched you," he snarled. "We saw you set out across our land!"

That was the noise I heard! "You've been following us," Tom said.

"A good thing we did," the man growled. "How dare you trample through Farmer Joss's cornfield?"

"We were being as careful as we could!" Elenna exclaimed. "You're doing far more damage with your feet!"

Tom gave Elenna a warning prod in the side. She was right, but there was no point in making their captors even angrier.

The men lifted the net off Tom and his friends and held long knives to their throats. They dragged Tom and Elenna down from Storm and bound their hands behind their backs. Silver growled and showed his teeth.

"No, boy," Elenna said. "Don't attack. We can't escape now."

Tom nodded. "Wait for a chance," he muttered to Elenna.

The men encircled them. "This way," their leader said.

He took Storm's bridle and led the horse towards the edge of the cornfield. The stallion didn't resist; he knew now was not the time to try to fight back.

The other men pushed Tom and Elenna after their leader. Silver padded alongside, keeping very close to Elenna. He seemed to understand that now wasn't the time to attack.

When they reached the other side of the cornfield, the men hustled them through a gate and along a road that led to the outskirts of a city, made up of paved roads and stone buildings.

This must be Meaton, Tom thought.

He heard the sound of distant voices as they passed along a street with tumbledown houses on either side. Soon they reached a square crowded with people.

The leader of the men began forcing his way through the crowd.

"Hey, Brandt," one of the townspeople hailed him, peering curiously at Tom and his friends. "What have you got there?"

"Trespassers," the leader called back. "We'll soon teach them a lesson."

The other man let out a short, harsh laugh. "We should let the wasps get at 'em."

Tom felt his heart thump harder at the mention of wasps, and he exchanged a glance with Elenna. *The Beast can't be far away!*

Brandt went on thrusting the crowd aside until they reached the centre of the square. There was a fountain there, shaped like a seahorse, but no water gushed from it, and the fountain's basin was dry and dusty. Beside it, Tom saw sweating men setting up stocks and nailing together makeshift cages from planks of wood.

"We can't let them put us in there," he whispered to Elenna. "We have to find the Beast – and quickly!"

The crowd pressed in all around them, a sea of furious faces with glaring eyes. Tom thought they looked like a pack of wild animals closing in on their prey.

"That's him!" a voice yelled. "It's all his fault!"

Tom spun around to see a man pushing his way to the front of the crowd. He recognised Jed, one of the miners from the Golden Valley in the North. Tom and Elenna had released them all from being Fang the bat fiend's slaves. But Jed didn't seem grateful for his freedom.

"This madness that grips the kingdom – it's all because of him," the miner went on, pushing his forefinger into Tom's chest. "He flooded the mines which provided all our wealth!"

"You've got it all wrong!" Tom retorted, struggling to free his hands from the cords that cut into his wrists. "You were blind in there, and terrified of the giant bat. We defeated Fang! We brought you *out* of the mine!"

But the crowd were shouting so loudly that Tom's voice was drowned out.

A burly man with an eyepatch shoved forward to stand beside Jed. Tom's heart sank as he recognised him – and the deadly throwing stars tucked into his belt.

"That's the man who tried to kill Silver for his pelt," Elenna hissed into Tom's ear. "The one we met when we were battling Murk."

Tom gritted his teeth as he summoned all his strength, but still couldn't loosen his bonds. Fear and anger were battling inside him. *I'm here to save my mother,* he thought desperately. *I need to find the Beast, before it's too late!*

But he knew that even if he told the citizens of Meaton about his Quest, they wouldn't believe him.

"We should execute the boy," the burly man called out. "He's brought nothing but trouble."

"No, take him to the queen!" another voice shouted.

I wish you would, Tom thought. *The queen would listen to us*.

"That's no good," a woman argued. She shook a long kitchen knife in Tom's face. "The kingdom is falling apart, and Queen Romaine can't do a thing to stop it. She can't even get rid of the plague of wasps!"

Wasps! Tom saw his own urgency reflected in Elenna's face. *That's the second time they have been mentioned.*

"Oof!" Tom let out a cry as a hard blow landed on the side of his head, knocking him to the ground. Darkness whirled round him as he felt himself being dragged over the cobblestones.

Tom tried to stand, but someone

was holding him down. As his vision cleared, he spotted another man approaching. He was tall and muscular, wearing a leather jerkin and leather bands around his wrists. He carried a long whip in his hand; its strands of knotted hide trailed along the ground.

Tom struggled to throw off the man who was holding him, but the blow had left him weak. Pain stabbed his head and the faces of his captors drifted in and out of focus.

Somewhere out of sight he could hear Elenna shouting in protest: "Let him go!"

The crowd cheered as the man with the whip cracked it against the ground a few times. He was grinning, as if he was looked forward to what he was going to do. Tom made a last effort to free himself, to get up and fight back, but pain was throbbing steadily through his head and his muscles wouldn't obey him.

Tom closed his eyes and braced himself as he saw the man raise his whip.

Here comes the pain...

CHAPTER THREE

THE DARKEST HOUR

Tom waited for the whip to strike, but nothing happened. A hush had fallen on the crowd. Opening his eyes, Tom saw them all gaping at the man with the whip. Instead of the stout handle with its leather thong, the Kayonian held a long, slithery snake with shining green scales; it coiled up in his hands and hissed into his face.

The man's eyes bulged with fear and shock. He screamed and dropped the snake, which raised its head and flicked its forked tongue angrily. The crowd backed away, terrified, shoving each other in their haste to get away from the deadly fangs.

"The boy's a sorcerer!" someone shouted.

"Leave him alone – he'll kill us all!" another voice added.

Tom watched, still dazed by the blow and amazed by the way the whip had changed to a snake. The panicking crowd ran off in every direction, vanishing down the streets that led into the square. Tom was left alone, with Elenna, Storm and Silver close by.

Then Tom noticed Wizard Aduro's young apprentice walking towards him. "Marc!" he exclaimed.

Sitting up, Tom realised that the bonds around his wrists had vanished. Elenna was free, too. She led Storm and Silver over to Marc, smiling in welcome. "It's so good to see you! How did you turn the whip into a snake?"

Marc returned her smile. He stretched out a hand towards the snake, which was still hissing and coiling along the ground, and spoke a single word under his breath. The snake immediately stretched out, stiffening. Its green scales changed to rough brown bark, and it became a wooden staff which flew into Marc's hand.

"Thank you for helping us," Tom said, struggling to his feet. The blow to his head had made his headache a hundred times worse, and he had to will his legs to stop shaking.

This is no good for a Beast Quest! he thought.

"Kayonia has entered its darkest hour," Marc said as Tom limped over to join him. "Chaos rampages through the city. Queen Romaine is trapped in her castle, besieged by the wasps. I can protect her for a time, Tom, but Vespick the wasp queen will conquer Meaton unless you and Elenna can do something about it."

A surge of energy flooded through Tom at the young wizard's words. "What are we waiting for?" he asked, straightening up. "To the castle!"

"That's the quickest way," Marc explained, pointing to a wide street which led away from the far side of the square. "I'll go on ahead and see what I can do to help."

A bright blue light flared up around the young wizard, and when it died away he was gone.

"Let's hurry," Tom said to Elenna. "While there's blood in my veins, I'll keep on fighting to save Kayonia!"

Tom and Elenna mounted Storm and galloped up the street with Silver bounding behind. As they approached Meaton, Tom was aware of people peering at him from behind window shutters, but no one tried to stop him. He guessed that they were too scared to venture outside.

A few small wasps buzzed between the houses, weaving a pattern against the sky.

At last the street led into another, bigger square. It was deserted; a row of abandoned market stalls stood at one side. The paving stones were littered with rubbish that stirred gently in the breeze.

The turrets of the castle rose across the square, outlined against a scarlet sky as the sun began to dip.

"I might have expected this," Tom

muttered, rage swelling inside him. "Just when we need daylight most!"

They reached the castle moat as the sun was swallowed by the horizon. Moonlight reflected in the glassy water.

The castle gates were open but there was no sign of any guards.

But when Tom urged Storm towards the drawbridge across the moat, a light flared up on the battlements.

"There's a torch!" Elenna cried out.

While she was still speaking, more torches appeared, one by one, until the castle was bathed in the eerie orange light of the flames.

"I'm sure we have Marc to thank for that," Tom said. "Now we can see to defeat the Beast."

As he and Elenna slid down from

Storm and looked around, Tom felt waves of heat against his cheeks.

The air was filled with an angry buzzing sound. "Look up there!" Elenna exclaimed. She pointed up at the tallest turret.

Tom gasped as he looked up. He'd never seen so many wasps in all his life. They hovered around the turret, and seemed to be encasing it in a huge globe of twigs, leaves and mud.

"What are they doing?" he asked.

Marc stepped forward from the shadows under the eaves of a nearby house. "They are building a wasps' nest," he replied.

"But – it's so big!" Elenna said, her eyes round with astonishment.

"There are hundreds of thousands of wasps here," Marc told her. "They are using the nest to imprison Queen

Romaine. I have protected her with a magical barrier, but she cannot move out of the turret."

Through the nest, Tom could see the shadow of the queen, jabbing at the inner wall of the nest with a long staff as she fought to free herself. But there were too many wasps, flying up with more mud and twigs to repair the holes she made. Even though the wasps sent a shiver of horror running through him, Tom couldn't help but be impressed by their application and skill.

"The queen won't be trapped for long," he vowed, clenching his fists. "That nest will be destroyed, if I have anything to do with it!"

"We'll have problems getting through the wasps," Elenna pointed out. "They'll fly down and sting us as soon as they know we're here."

"I can use my magic to make a shield to protect you while you enter the castle," Marc replied. "That will cover you until you can reach the queen. Her people need her to fight back. But you must be quick."

"Maybe we should tackle Vespick first," Elenna suggested. "It will be easier to save the queen once we're sure the Beast is vanquished."

Tom thought for a moment, then shook his head. "I can't leave the queen in that kind of danger," he said, glancing up again at the monstrous nest. "The Quest can wait – for a little while."

CHAPTER FOUR

VESPICK!

Tom leapt back into Storm's saddle and Elenna scrambled up behind him. Marc reached out his hands and began to whisper an incantation. As Tom urged Storm forwards, he saw a faint silver-blue bubble form around them. It gave out a pleasant warmth, like a spring breeze.

Encouraging Storm into a gallop, Tom raced down the street towards the drawbridge and the castle gate beyond, with Silver scampering along behind them. As they approached the gate, countless wasps hurtled down. Tom heard their furious buzzing as they bounced off the shield Marc had conjured.

Behind him, he felt Elenna shudder. "It's a good thing we have Marc to help us."

Tom scanned the sky for signs of Vespick.

Where is this Beast? he thought.

Storm's hooves echoed on the rickety drawbridge as he galloped across the moat surrounding the castle. Tom guided Storm under the archway and they burst into a vast hall. Two rows of pillars stretched high up into the shadows of a vaulted roof. More torches were burning on the walls, lighting up the rich tapestries that hung around the hall.

There was still no sign of any guards, though discarded weapons and pieces of armour littered the floor.

There was a fight here, Tom thought.

Elenna leapt nimbly from the saddle. At that moment, the warmth of the shimmering blue globe that had protected Tom and his friends turned suddenly cold, and the light flickered and died.

"Close the door!" Tom shouted.

Elenna raced back across the hall and slammed the door shut on the swarms of wasps that were pursuing them.

"That was close!" Tom exclaimed.

One or two wasps had made it into the hall before the doors were shut, but they flew harmlessly up to the roof, high above Tom's head.

"We're safe for the moment," Tom went on. "Now we need to find the way to the turret and..."

His voice trailed off as he realised that he could still hear a low buzzing sound.

"What's that?" Elenna asked, hearing it at the same time. "We left the swarm outside. Where's the noise coming from?"

Tom looked in the direction of the sound as it grew louder. Icy horror trickled down his spine as his gaze fell on the throne at the far end of the hall. It was made of carved wood, covered with gold and glittering with jewels. Seated on it was a huge creature, twice as tall as a man. The upper part of its body was human, except for its wasp-like head with its bulging eyes; the lower half was a slender wasp body, covered in stripes of black and gold. It ended in a long, sharp sting that glowed with a green light. The creature had six strong limbs that ended in cruel, hooked claws. Four wings sprouted from its back; they whirred gently, making the buzzing sound.

"Vespick," Tom said hoarsely.

Never taking his eyes off the Beast, Tom unhooked his shield from its place on the saddle, and drew his sword.

"Come and fight!" he challenged. "Let's see how strong you are!"

As he spoke, the Wasp Queen lifted off from the throne, her wings a silver blur as she hovered above the ground. Her buzzing was so loud that the torches on the pillars began to shake, their flames whipping to and fro. Tom's ears itched with discomfort as the sound drilled into his head.

Tom could hear Elenna behind him, ready to back him up. Giving a quick glance over his shoulder, he saw that instead of her bow she held a long, curved sword that gleamed in the torchlight.

That must be one of the swords the guards dropped, he thought. *But what happened to them?*

There was no time to ponder. Vespick flew high up into the vaults, then launched herself into a long dive towards Tom. The buzzing of her wings rose to a high-pitched, threatening whine.

Storm whinnied nervously and stamped his hooves, the sound ringing from the hall's stone floor. Silver let out a low snarl, baring his teeth as if he was going to attack the Wasp Queen along with Tom.

"No, boy. Get back!" Elenna warned him.

Tom held his shield up to protect himself, gripping his sword, aiming for the Beast's eyes.

This is it...

CHAPTER FIVE

THE SWARM

Tom dug his heels into Storm's flank, urging him forwards. They charged down the hall to meet the Beast, the stallion's hooves ringing on the stone floor. As the Wasp Queen reached out to grab Tom with her vicious, swiping claws, Tom ducked and felt the draught of her body ruffle his hair as she swept overhead.

He swung his sword at her belly

but the blade passed harmlessly through the Beast's armour. One of Vespick's wings slapped down hard at his sword arm, knocking the blade out of his hand.

At that moment, Tom felt a sharp blow on his back. Pain stabbed through him. He lost his balance and went flying from the saddle, hitting the floor on his front with a hard thump.

Dazed, the breath driven out of him, Tom scrambled to recover his sword, expecting at any moment to feel the Beast's cruel claws slicing into his back. He heard Elenna shout a battle cry and saw her swinging her new sword at the Wasp Queen. She stood over Tom, stopping Vespick from attacking him while he was helpless. Silver leapt into the air, growling and snarling, trying to reach the Beast.

Heartened by his friends' courage, Tom grabbed his sword and jumped to his feet again. He fixed his eyes on the Beast's sharp sting which glowed a sinister green; yellowish poison dripped from it, splashing stickily on the floor.

That could be the last ingredient for the potion to save my mother, Tom guessed with a fresh surge of hope. *I have to get it!* He raised his sword, waiting for Vespick as she swooped down on him again. *If I can just time my swing right...*

Thwack! As the Wasp Queen hovered above Tom, she twisted her lithe body around. Tom saw the blow coming and flung up his shield in time to block her claws, but the force of it sent him skidding across the floor again.

In the same movement, Vespick whipped round and lashed out with one of her mighty legs, kicking Elenna in the face. Letting out a sharp cry, Elenna went flying backwards. She crashed into the hall doors. They burst open and Elenna landed on the narrow strip of ground between the castle and the moat.

Silver gave a furious howl and raced after her.

Tom shook his head to clear it and saw wasps swarm through the open door, filling it from the roof to the floor. They danced around their Queen in such a dense swarm that Tom could hardly see her.

He struggled to his feet and groped his way through the swirl of wasps until he reached Storm. The black stallion was stamping his hooves on the floor, tossing his head and lashing his tail as he tried to dislodge the wasps that were crawling over his coat, driving their stings into him.

"Come on, boy," Tom muttered as he grabbed the reins. "Let's get out of here."

Leading the frightened horse, Tom guided him out of the hall and towards Elenna as fast as he could.

His friend was just getting up. Silver was nuzzling at her, whining softly. Elenna rested a hand on his head to reassure him. "Don't worry," she gasped. "I'm all right."

Before Tom could reach them, the wasps inside the hall swarmed out again, surrounding Tom and Elenna and buzzing in a fury as they attacked with their sharp stings. Tom swung his sword at them but they danced out of the way of the blade. He felt as if his skin was on fire from countless tiny wounds.

The crowd of wasps thickened, blotting out Elenna and Silver from Tom's sight. He could hear Silver howling in pain and Elenna's voice raised in a shout.

"Tom! What can we do?"

Tom couldn't reply. *We have to get rid of these wasps before we can attack the Beast,* he thought. *But how?*

CHAPTER SIX

SMOKED OUT!

Tom spun around at the sound of an even louder buzzing, to see Vespick hurtling towards the doors of the hall.

No! I can't fight her and the swarm at the same time.

An arrow swished past and ricocheted off the Beast's wing. Elenna came to Tom's side, swatting wasps out of the way. His friend had slid the sword into her belt and unslung her bow. She loosed another shaft at the Wasp Queen. This one also bounced off Vespick's body, but the Beast slowed down. Elenna loosed arrow after arrow to hold the Beast at bay, but Tom could see her quiver would soon be empty.

We need a better plan, he thought, brushing the wasps from his face.

Buzzing with frustration, Vespick retreated into the hall again.

"Well done!" Tom called to Elenna. But as he spoke, a cloud of wasps attacked with renewed energy. He staggered to and fro, looking around desperately through the seething swarm. At first he couldn't see anything that would help. Then he noticed a brick building attached to the west side of the castle. Through the open door he could see a fire burning, and a blacksmith's anvil and tools.

A forge! In spite of the pain from the wasp stings, Tom grinned. *I grew up in a forge. I know exactly how it can help us.*

"Follow me!" he shouted to Elenna. "Trust me, I know what to do."

He led Storm over to the forge, with Elenna and Silver behind him. The forge had a brick-built chimney stack, with thick plumes of black smoke gently swirling out of the top. Metal piping ran along the outside walls, before disappearing inside the hearth.

Tom turned to Elenna as she came up to him, flapping her hands in front of her face in an effort to keep the wasps away.

"I know you haven't had that sword very long," he said to her, "but do you think you could help me make holes in the piping? If we can get the smoke to pour out in all directions, it should drive away these small wasps."

Elenna let out a yelp as another of the wasps stung her hand. "You just watch me!" she replied, her eyes shining with determination as she drew the sword again.

Standing side by side, Tom and Elenna hacked at the metal pipes, taking it in turns to chop at the same spot. Sparks flew as their blades clanged off the iron surface; soon they had made a large dent, then a deep gash in the pipe. Thick black smoke gushed out in swirling plumes.

Tom coughed as the smoke clogged his throat. He pulled up the front of his tunic to cover his mouth and nose. Elenna did the same with a fold of her cloak. Ducking down, they stumbled away from the hole in the pipe where the smoke was pouring out. They crossed the drawbridge into the square to get away from the worst of it.

Soon Tom heard a light pattering on the stones of the square, and he realised that the wasps were beginning to fall out of the sky. Tom's face burned from the stings.

But there was still a bigger foe to face.

"It's working!" Elenna gazed around in wonderment. Her face was covered in red blotches. "Are the wasps dead?"

“No, the smoke is putting them to sleep,” Tom said. “Let’s hope they stay that way until I’ve had a chance to defeat the Beast!”

The first light drizzle of wasps became a heavy rain as the smoke overcame them and they fell to the ground, heaping up all around Tom and Elenna. Silver sniffed one of the nearest heaps and snorted in disgust.

"Silver, don't even *think* of eating any of those!" Elenna chided.

Tom patted Storm's neck to calm him, and ran his fingers through the stallion's mane to comb out any stray wasps lodged there.

Before long, the Kayonian sky was clear of wasps. Tom and Elenna stood at a safe distance from the smoke. Tom ran the talon of Epos the Flame Bird, which he kept on his shield, over his companions' stings to heal them, then did the same to himself.

"Now I'm ready to face the Beast," he said.

"Is she still in the hall?" Elenna asked. "I wonder if the smoke got that far. The Wasp Queen might be asleep, too."

Before she finished speaking, a terrible droning noise came from the open door of the hall.

"I think that answers your question," Tom said grimly. "Vespick's wide awake. And she's *angry*!"

CHAPTER SEVEN

A NEW ALLY

Tom heard a voice calling out to him from somewhere up above. "Wait, I'm coming. I'll help you!"

He looked up to the top of the turret where the wasps had imprisoned Queen Romaine in their nest.

Now that the smoke had sent the swarm to sleep, Queen Romaine was kicking and punching at the walls of the nest. Holes appeared in the sides, sending scraps of twig and mud hailing down into the moat.

But Queen Romaine was still not free when the Wasp Queen launched herself out through the doors of the hall, her eyes blazing.

Tom brandished his sword. "Come on!" he yelled. "I'm ready for you!"

The Beast charged through the air, straight at Tom and Elenna. Tom pushed Elenna one way and dived the other. Vespick whirled to pursue his friend, her wings a blur as she homed in on her target.

Fear surged through Tom as he realised how fast his enemy was, and she could attack with her clawed limbs, her wings, or her sting.

How can I defeat her?

Elenna ducked as Vespick swiped at

her with her wings; she retaliated by stabbing her sword at the creature's underside as the Beast flew over her head. Vespick screeched and twisted away.

Tom leapt up on Vespick's blind side and tried to slash at one of her claws. But the Wasp Queen spun in the air and thrust her deadly sting at him. He jumped away again, staggering to keep his balance as he felt the blast of her wings smash into his shield.

Her wings...

Tom realised that the Wasp Queen's swift flight was giving her the advantage. *If I can only cut off her wings...*

But he couldn't see how to get close to her wings when she was hovering in the air above him. She made sure that she never turned her back to Tom or Elenna, and brandished her clawed arms like eagle's talons.

Scraps of the wasps' nest were still raining down from above as Queen Romaine battled for her freedom.

Some of them struck Vespick, but the Wasp Queen shook them off. She swooped down on Tom and Elenna, fury in her bulging eyes, her yellow and black body bristling. Tom dodged into the cover between the castle wall and one of the abandoned market stalls, dragging Elenna behind him.

"This isn't working," Elenna gasped. "We've got to find the Beast's weakness."

For a moment Tom couldn't think clearly. He heard Vespick battering against the market stall, her angry buzzing rising again to a high-pitched whine. Soon the flimsy framework would collapse under her blows.

Tom peered out at the Wasp Queen, ducking under his shield. He suddenly remembered something. Hope sprang up inside him.

Maybe there is a way…

"Elenna, can you keep the Beast distracted?" he asked.

"I'll try!" his friend replied.

"I want you to lure her underneath the turret window," Tom told her, pointing to where Queen Romaine had been imprisoned. The rain of nest scraps had stopped falling.

Does that mean the queen is free?

Tom had no time to think about that now. "Go!" he told Elenna.

His friend sprang out of the cover of the stall. As Vespick swooped down on her again, she flung herself aside, rolled and nimbly sprang up onto her feet again, heading for the turret.

Once the Wasp Queen had gone, Tom raced back into the castle and headed for a spiral staircase that led up from the hall.

This must lead to the north turret, he thought.

As he climbed up into the gloom, he saw the glint of a weapon ahead. It sliced through the air; Tom barely brought his own sword up in time to parry it. The clash of steel jarred his arm and he fell back. He saw the outline of his attacker, wielding a bone staff in one hand, a sword in the other.

"Wait!" Tom gasped. "I'm here to help."

His attacker retreated slightly up the steps, and in the light from a torch set in the wall, Tom saw that he was face-to-face with Queen Romaine of Kayonia. She was a tall woman with a fierce, pale face, and copper-coloured hair tumbling over her shoulders. She slowly lowered her sword and staff as she gazed at Tom.

"Who are you?" she asked. "And what are you doing in my castle?"

"I'm a friend from Avantia," Tom explained rapidly. "I've come to help you."

"I saw how you cleared the sky of the wasps that were attacking us," the Queen said. "Now I must try to rid my people of the fear that has them in its grip. Whoever you are, young warrior, whatever you are planning, I wish you luck."

"Thank you," Tom replied, impressed by the Queen's courage. "I promise you, I will never give up until this Beast is defeated."

As Tom finished speaking, the sound of buzzing filled his ears again. At first he thought that Vespick must have followed him up the stairs. Then he realised that this new sound came from every direction at once. "Oh no!" he exclaimed. "The wasps have woken up!"

Queen Romaine sheathed her sword and snatched a torch from the wall. She pushed past Tom to descend the stairs. Pausing to look back at him, she said, "I will rally my people with more torches and smoke, to drive off the swarm. The Beast is your task."

Tom looked after the Queen as she ran down the stairs, the flame of the torch streaming out behind her. "Don't worry!" he called. "While there's blood in my veins, the Wasp Queen will not win!"

CHAPTER EIGHT

COMBAT IN THE SKY

Tom climbed up the stairs until he reached the room at the top of the turret. Mud, twigs and leaves from the nest littered the floor, along with the bodies of dead wasps.

Barely glancing at them, Tom ran across the room and squeezed out of the narrow window. Perching on the ledge outside, he looked down into the square. The moat and the drawbridge looked tiny, and the rooftops of the city stretched all around.

Far below, Elenna had mounted Storm and was guiding the stallion up and down, not far from the end of the drawbridge, pursued by the raging Beast. Vespick swooped low over the ground, swiping at Elenna with her arms and her sting, while Elenna cleverly turned Storm this way and that, slashing at the Wasp Queen with her sword. Silver darted in close to Vespick, snapping at her limbs, then springing away again before the Beast could reach him with her raking claws.

Fear stabbed through Tom as he spotted the horde of wasps rising up again around Elenna. So far, she hadn't noticed them. Tom knew she would be in real trouble when the swarm started attacking her, too.

Tom saw Romaine run out of the castle into the square, her torch held high. He took a deep breath. *It's time.*

Holding his shield above his head, Tom leapt from the window of the turret. His stomach lurched as he plummeted through the air. Then Arcta's eagle feather, fixed in his shield, slowed his fall; he drifted gently down to where Vespick still darted after Elenna.

Tom angled the shield to catch the breeze so that he floated over the Wasp Queen. Vespick did not notice him until he landed on her back with a thud. Her whole body arched and she thrashed this way and that as she tried to throw Tom off. Tom gripped her armoured neck and held on, determined not to lose his advantage. He caught a glimpse of Elenna staring at him in amazement; she narrowed her eyes as the wasp swarm swirled around her.

"Look after yourself!" he shouted. "I'll handle Vespick!"

Tom clung even tighter as the Wasp Queen launched herself into the air, writhing in her efforts to get rid of her unwanted rider.

That's right, he thought to himself. *Fly as high as you want. Your fall will hurt you all the more.*

Vespick flew high into the air. Tom's knuckles were white as he was carried past the window of the turret from which he had leapt only moments before. On her way over the battlements, Vespick battered Tom against the stones, trying to dislodge him. Tom gritted his teeth against the pain and gripped even harder.

Vespick spiralled up, high above the castle. The moat was a circle, gleaming orange in the torchlight. But Tom had no time to admire the view. Vespick flipped upside down, and Tom squeezed his legs against her side to hold on. "You won't get rid of me that easily!" he shouted over the drone of her wings. His head spun as the castle and the sky whirled dizzily past.

To his relief, Vespick righted herself. Down in the square, Tom could see Elenna, small as a toy figure, fending off the swarm of wasps with her whirling sword. Marc stood beside her, moving his arms as he cast magic.

In the castle gateway, Queen Romaine was calling to her people. Tom could see some of the citizens of Meaton throwing open the doors of their houses and running up to answer her command. As she gestured towards them, they grabbed the magical torches from the castle walls and brandished them at the wasp swarm.

Tom's heart thumped hard with triumph. *The tide is turning! We can win this battle!*

Keeping a firm grip with one hand, he unsheathed his sword and hacked at Vespick's wings. Despite their flimsy appearance, they were tough as old leather. The Wasp Queen's body spasmed in pain, but she couldn't reach Tom to make him stop. She aimed her sting at him, curving it over her back. The deadly spike still dripped with its thick, yellowish poison, and Tom flinched away.

He aimed blow after blow at the Wasp Queen's wings. As the right set came loose, Vespick lurched violently to one side. Tom saw the wing flutter

down into the square.

With his jaw set in determination, he began hacking at the second wing. Vespick's buzzing faltered and she bucked in a last effort to throw Tom off. As the Beast lost her left wing, she began spiralling clumsily out of control.

The Beast let out a shriek of fear and anger as she plummeted down.

Tom felt air rushing past his face as he fell with her.

This is the end of the Wasp Queen...

CHAPTER NINE

FREYA IN DANGER

Tom barely had time to jump off Vespick's back and hold up his shield with Arcta's feather to slow his fall. Vespick hit the castle moat, sending a geyser of dank water splashing everywhere.

Tom drifted down. "Let's hope she's gone for good," he muttered to himself as the Wasp Queen sank out of sight. The castle walls slid past him as his shield bore him safely to the ground.

All that was left of Vespick was her glowing green sting, floating on the water. Elenna knelt on the edge of the moat, grasped the fearsome spike, then ran up to Tom, a wide grin on her face. The sting was as long as the sword in her other hand, and looked just as deadly. Silver bounded at her side, with Storm trotting behind.

"It's a good thing you came when you did," Elenna said. "I wasn't sure how long I could hold Vespick off."

"Long enough," Tom said. "You did well with that sword."

Elenna swished the sword through the air, watching torchlight gleam on the blade. "I think I'll keep it – as long as you promise to teach me some moves."

"I'll be happy to," Tom replied. "Just as soon as we—"

An evil laugh rang out through the air, interrupting Tom. Tom and Elenna froze at the sound.

They looked up. A tall figure stood on the north turret, amidst the ruins of the wasps' nest. Velmal! The evil wizard was surrounded by a sphere of sickly purple light.

"You're defeated!" Tom shouted defiantly. "Kayonia is free of your curse!"

"Defeated?" Velmal cackled. "By you, Avantian? You may have destroyed my Beasts, but aren't you forgetting something?"

The evil wizard held out his arms and Freya's body appeared, slumped over them, her legs and arms dangling. Her face was turned towards Tom; she was pale as death and her eyes were closed.

"Mother!" Tom gasped.

Velmal nodded, a grim smile on his face. "If you want your mother so much, you can have her..."

Velmal's form shimmered and faded away. The purple light vanished. Nothing was left to hold Freya up and she plunged down from the tower, straight towards the murky water of the moat.

"No!" Tom yelled. Panic surged through him. He darted forwards, but he was too far away to help his mother.

A heartbeat before she hit the water, a wave of pale blue light enveloped Freya's falling body, suspending her in the air. Tom spun around to see that the light was shining from Marc's outstretched hands, as the young wizard murmured a spell.

Marc guided Freya over to Tom and Elenna and set her gently down on the ground. Tom flung himself to his knees beside his mother and gathered her up into his arms.

Elenna crouched beside Tom. "Will she be all right?" she asked anxiously.

Tom looked down into his mother's face. Freya's eyes were closed. She didn't seem to be in pain any more, but she felt heavy, and when Tom shook her gently, she didn't wake. She didn't even seem to be breathing.

"You can't be dead," Tom said hoarsely. "Please don't be dead."

He couldn't believe that his Quest would end like this. He had travelled through two strange kingdoms, meeting every challenge that Velmal had set him. He had defeated fearsome Beasts, and collected all the ingredients to make the magic healing potion. His mother couldn't die now, not when he had everything he needed to save her.

"Wake up," Tom begged in an

agonised whisper. "Please wake up..."

Marc staggered over to stand beside them. Tom could see from his shaking limbs that using so much magic had drained him.

"Is my mother dead?" Tom asked, his voice trembling with grief. "Isn't there anything we can do?"

Marc looked down gravely at Freya. "I will try my best," he said. "But there's no telling how deep Velmal's evil magic has gone."

With a grunt of effort, Marc held his hands apart, and a cauldron slowly formed between them. Tom looked inside, to see all the other Kayonian ingredients that he had collected on his Quests: the pearl, the red jewel, the jade ring, the chain of weeds, and the flower.

"Here's Vespick's sting," Elenna

said, handing the long spike to Marc.

Marc took the sting and placed it into the cauldron, then muttered a magical charm in a language Tom didn't recognise.

Almost immediately, a faint wisp of blue steam rose from the cauldron. Glancing inside again, Tom saw that the ingredients had vanished, to be replaced by a sludgy blue liquid. Bubbles formed and popped on the surface.

The liquid began to froth, threatening to spill over the rim. The wisp of blue steam became a thick plume. With a wave of his hand, Marc directed the vapour towards Freya's face. It seemed to sink into her skin and sail up her nostrils.

Tom watched anxiously. Nothing happened. He felt tears well up in his eyes. His last hope was gone. His mother was dead.

Then Freya's eyelashes quivered. Tom drew in a long, shaky breath, hardly able to believe what he was seeing. "Mother?" he murmured.

Freya's eyes opened. Colour began to return to her pale cheeks. A moment later she sat up, smiling weakly. "My son..." she whispered.

CHAPTER TEN

THE BLACK FLAG

There were so many questions Tom wanted to ask. *Who are you? Where are you from, and how did you meet my father, Taladon? Why did you leave Avantia*?

But there was only one question that mattered now. "Mother, are you all right?"

Freya smiled. "I will be, now that I

have been restored. And I owe it all to you, my son."

As Tom's mother spoke, Queen Romaine appeared, a torch still gripped in one hand, her staff in the other. Tom scrambled to his feet and gave his hand to Freya to pull her up. Both of them bowed to the Queen.

"Well done," Romaine said, inclining her head to Tom. "You have my thanks."

"I did what I had to, Your Majesty," Tom replied.

"Now I have another duty for you," Queen Romaine went on. "The people here are waiting to hear me address them. I would like you to come with me."

Tom and Elenna followed Queen Romaine across the drawbridge and back into the castle. She led them up a stairway and out onto a high balcony. They stood at the back with Marc and Freya while Romaine stepped forward to address her people, who had gathered in the square below.

Silver padded out behind Elenna. "Quiet, boy," she murmured, resting a hand on his head.

"People of Kayonia!" Queen Romaine began. "Our kingdom has been through a destructive time. I know that some of you have blamed me, but I assure you that our troubles were caused by the evil wizard Velmal. Now he has been defeated, thanks to the help of heroes from Avantia."

As the Queen stepped back to point at Tom, Elenna and Marc, the whole crowd in the square erupted into cheering. Tom felt himself flush with embarrassment as he bowed.

Queen Romaine raised her hand and gradually the cheers died away. "The task of rebuilding our kingdom now begins," she announced. "None of those who tried to rebel against me will be punished. You were deceived, but now you all know the truth. Together we will restore Kayonia, so that it is stronger than ever before."

Tom was impressed by the Queen's words. She was obviously a capable ruler, like King Hugo of Avantia. He was sure that Kayonia would recover quickly under her leadership. He was just glad that now he could go home to—

Tom's shield was tugged from his shoulder. "What—?" he began, stunned, as he saw his mother Freya swinging it around.

Before Tom could react, Freya thrust herself in front of him, holding up the shield to block a beam of purple light, which bounced off it and spilled harmlessly over the castle wall.

"Dark magic!" Marc exclaimed.

Tom, Elenna and Freya sprang forward to look over the balcony. Down below in the main square, a hooded figure emerged from the crowd. The Kayonian people scattered away from him in panic.

"Velmal!" Tom exclaimed.

The evil wizard pulled back his hood to reveal his cold, sneering face. "You thought I was defeated?" he called out. "Think again!"

As he raised his staff to release another bolt of magic, Tom drew his sword. Freya grabbed it from him. "No!" she told him. "This is *my* battle."

Bearing Tom's sword and shield, Freya leapt from the balcony, flipping over in a somersault. She landed, graceful as a cat, in the square, a few paces from Velmal. The evil wizard threw another bolt of purple light at her as she advanced on him, but Freya deflected it with the shield.

Tom stood, gripping the balcony rail as he looked on. He could hardly bear to watch, but he couldn't take his eyes off his mother.

"I could have fought Velmal," he muttered. "Why did my mother have to go into danger? Velmal *can't* kill her now, not when we've just found each other!"

Elenna put a hand comfortingly on his arm. "She'll be all right. She has to punish Velmal for what he did to her."

Below, the people of Meaton crowded at the edges of the square. They yelled encouragement as Freya reached Velmal. The wizard's purple light grew fainter and faded away, as if his magic was exhausted. He swiped with his staff, but Freya swung Tom's sword, shattering the staff to splinters.

The sneer vanished from Velmal's face, to be replaced with pale fear. The wizard backed away from Freya, but she followed him determinedly and brought Tom's sword around in a fierce slash.

The blade struck, shearing through Velmal's body at the waist, cutting him in half. A shriek of pain tore from the wizard's throat and a heartbeat later he exploded in an explosion of purple sparks.

Tom let out a cheer, echoed by all the people in the square. "She did it!" Tom yelled. "Velmal is destroyed forever!"

The Kayonian people crowded around Freya, lifting her onto their shoulders. Tom gazed down with pride as his mother was carried back in triumph towards the castle.

"It's all over!" Elenna sighed happily. "And now we can go home!"

Tom gripped her shoulder. "At last!" he agreed. "Sometimes I wondered if we'd ever see Avantia again."

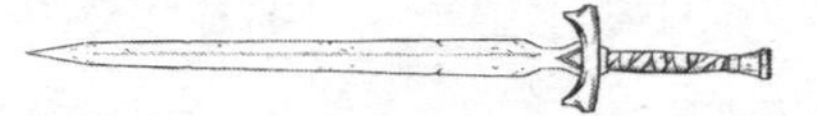

Next morning, Tom, his mother and Elenna stood in the great hall of the castle. Tom held Storm by his bridle, while Silver stood quietly by Elenna's side.

The night before, Queen Romaine had held a feast there, with music and dancing, to celebrate the death of Velmal. At last, Tom had been able to sit beside his mother and ask her questions and tell her about what he had faced on his Beast Quest.

Now the hall was empty. In the

middle, Marc had conjured a portal, a tall gateway of shimmering blue light. Through it, Tom could see the green hills of Avantia, with clouds scudding across a blue sky. A longing for his own country surged through him, and he exchanged a happy glance with Elenna.

"I can't wait to see everyone again," Elenna said. "King Hugo and Wizard Aduro, and your father and uncle and aunt, Tom."

Before Tom could reply, Queen Romaine stepped forward. "Kayonia will always be in your debt," she said. "Ask what you will of me, and it is yours."

Tom bowed to the Queen, his heart swelling with gratitude. "Thank you, Your Majesty," he replied. "But I have all I want. My mother returned to me, strong and unharmed."

He exchanged a glance with Freya, whose eyes were shining with love for him.

"Then I bid you farewell," Queen Romaine said. "And if Avantia needs help, then you may always call on Kayonia."

"Goodbye, Your Majesty." With another bow to the Queen, Tom led Storm into the portal. Elenna and Silver were by his side, with Marc and Freya just behind.

The blue light enveloped him. *Home at last!*

It had been so long since he had travelled the familiar roads of Avantia. He had faced so many Beasts and completed so many Quests since he left.

And this time I'm returning with my

mother, Tom thought joyfully. *The whole family will be together again, for the first time in my life.*

King Hugo's castle hovered mysteriously into view at the end of the tunnel of blue light. Tom quickened his pace as he gazed eagerly at the familiar walls and towers.

But before they reached the other side of the portal, Elenna stopped short. "The castle looks...different, somehow." Her voice sounded uneasy.

Tom stared at the battlements and turrets of the castle. At first he couldn't see what Elenna meant. Then his gaze fell on the topmost tower.

"I see it!" he exclaimed. "Why is there a black flag flying over King Hugo's castle?"

As he stared at the dark banner fluttering in the breeze, Tom drew a deep breath. *What has been happening since I left*?

Here's a sneak preview of Tom's next exciting adventure in the new Beast Quest series, The Lost World, coming soon!

Meet

CONVOL THE COLD-BLOODED BRUTE

Tom faces his greatest challenge yet! Can he defeat wicked Malvel, once and for all?

PROLOGUE

Dalaton puffed across to the far side of the courtyard where, near a rack of fearsome looking spears, stood two of his fellow guards.

"Looks like Dalaton the Swift is in a hurry!" one said.

"He's as quick as a hare fleeing a fox," laughed the other.

Dalaton waddled past, ignoring them. He wished his stomach was slightly less rotund, but he was used to the teasing. Some said a three-legged tortoise would beat him in a race!

He glanced over his shoulder and checked that the guards had turned back to their duties. Then he slipped away from prying eyes down a dark passage, unlit by torches.

You shouldn't be doing this, he told himself. *You should mind your own business. Go to bed!* But he kept on walking.

At the end of the passage, he pressed himself up against a wall. He tried to catch his breath, listening for any sounds. There was nothing, except for the distant neighing of a horse in the castle stables.

If I'm caught here, he thought, *the king will surely put me in chains. Or worse…*

Dalaton shuddered. There was no going back now. He peeped out from his hiding place towards the steps leading down to the dungeon. The good wizard Oradu was being held captive down there, and Dalaton wanted to help him.

But how? What can I do?

He crept to the top of the steps. A low moan drifted up, echoing off the dripping stone walls; perhaps he was too late. The other guards said the king was trying to steal Oradu's powers. Word was that Oradu's spellbook, cauldron and pet falcon had already been taken away from him.

Follow this Quest to the end in CONVOL THE COLD-BLOODED BRUTE.

Win an exclusive Beast Quest T-shirt and goody bag!

Tom has battled many fearsome Beasts and we want to know which one is your favourite! Send us a drawing or painting of your favourite Beast and tell us in 30 words why you think it's the best.

Each month we will select **three** winners to receive a Beast Quest T-shirt and goody bag!

Send your entry on a postcard to
BEAST QUEST COMPETITION
Orchard Books, 338 Euston Road, London NW1 3BH.

Australian readers should email:
childrens.books@hachette.com.au

New Zealand readers should write to:
Beast Quest Competition, PO Box 3255, Shortland St, Auckland 1140, NZ or email: childrensbooks@hachette.co.nz

Don't forget to include your name and address. Only one entry per child.

Good luck!

Fight the Beasts, Fear the Magic

www.beastquest.co.uk

Have you checked out the Beast Quest website? It's the place to go for games, downloads, activities, sneak previews and lots of fun!

You can read all about your favourite beasts, download free screensavers and desktop wallpapers for your computer, and even challenge your friends to a Beast Tournament.

Sign up to the newsletter at www.beastquest.co.uk to receive exclusive extra content and the opportunity to enter special members-only competitions. We'll send you up-to-date info on all the Beast Quest books, including the next exciting series which features four brand-new Beasts!

☐1.	Ferno the Fire Dragon	978 1 84616 483 5	4.99
☐2.	Sepron the Sea Serpent	978 1 84616 482 8	4.99
☐3.	Arcta the Mountain Giant	978 1 84616 484 2	4.99
☐4.	Tagus the Horse-Man	978 1 84616 486 6	4.99
☐5.	Nanook the Snow Monster	978 1 84616 485 9	4.99
☐6.	Epos the Flame Bird	978 1 84616 487 3	4.99

Beast Quest: The Golden Armour

☐7.	Zepha the Monster Squid	978 1 84616 988 5	4.99
☐8.	Claw the Giant Monkey	978 1 84616 989 2	4.99
☐9.	Soltra the Stone Charmer	978 1 84616 990 8	4.99
☐10.	Vipero the Snake Man	978 1 84616 991 5	4.99
☐11.	Arachnid the King of Spiders	978 1 84616 992 2	4.99
☐12.	Trillion the Three-Headed Lion	978 1 84616 993 9	4.99

Beast Quest: The Dark Realm

☐13.	Torgor the Minotaur	978 1 84616 997 7	4.99
☐14.	Skor the Winged Stallion	978 1 84616 998 4	4.99
☐15.	Narga the Sea Monster	978 1 40830 000 8	4.99
☐16.	Kaymon the Gorgon Hound	978 1 40830 001 5	4.99
☐17.	Tusk the Mighty Mammoth	978 1 40830 002 2	4.99
☐18.	Sting the Scorpion Man	978 1 40830 003 9	4.99

Beast Quest: The Amulet of Avantia

☐19.	Nixa the Death Bringer	978 1 40830 376 4	4.99
☐20.	Equinus the Spirit Horse	978 1 40830 377 1	4.99
☐21.	Rashouk the Cave Troll	978 1 40830 378 8	4.99
☐22.	Luna the Moon Wolf	978 1 40830 379 5	4.99
☐23.	Blaze the Ice Dragon	978 1 40830 381 8	4.99
☐24.	Stealth the Ghost Panther	978 1 40830 380 1	4.99

Beast Quest: The Shade of Death

☐25.	Krabb Master of the Sea	978 1 40830 437 2	4.99
☐26.	Hawkite Arrow of the Air	978 1 40830 438 9	4.99
☐27.	Rokk the Walking Mountain	978 1 40830 439 6	4.99
☐28.	Koldo the Arctic Warrior	978 1 40830 440 2	4.99
☐29.	Trema the Earth Lord	978 1 40830 441 9	4.99
☐30.	Amictus the Bug Queen	978 1 40830 442 6	4.99

Special Bumper Editions

☐Vedra & Krimon: Twin Beasts of Avantia	978 1 84616 951 9	5.99
☐Spiros the Ghost Phoenix	978 1 84616 994 6	5.99
☐Arax the Soul Stealer	978 1 40830 382 5	5.99
☐Kragos & Kildor: The Two-Headed Demon	978 1 40830 436 5	5.99
☐Creta the Winged Terror	978 1 40830 735 9	5.99

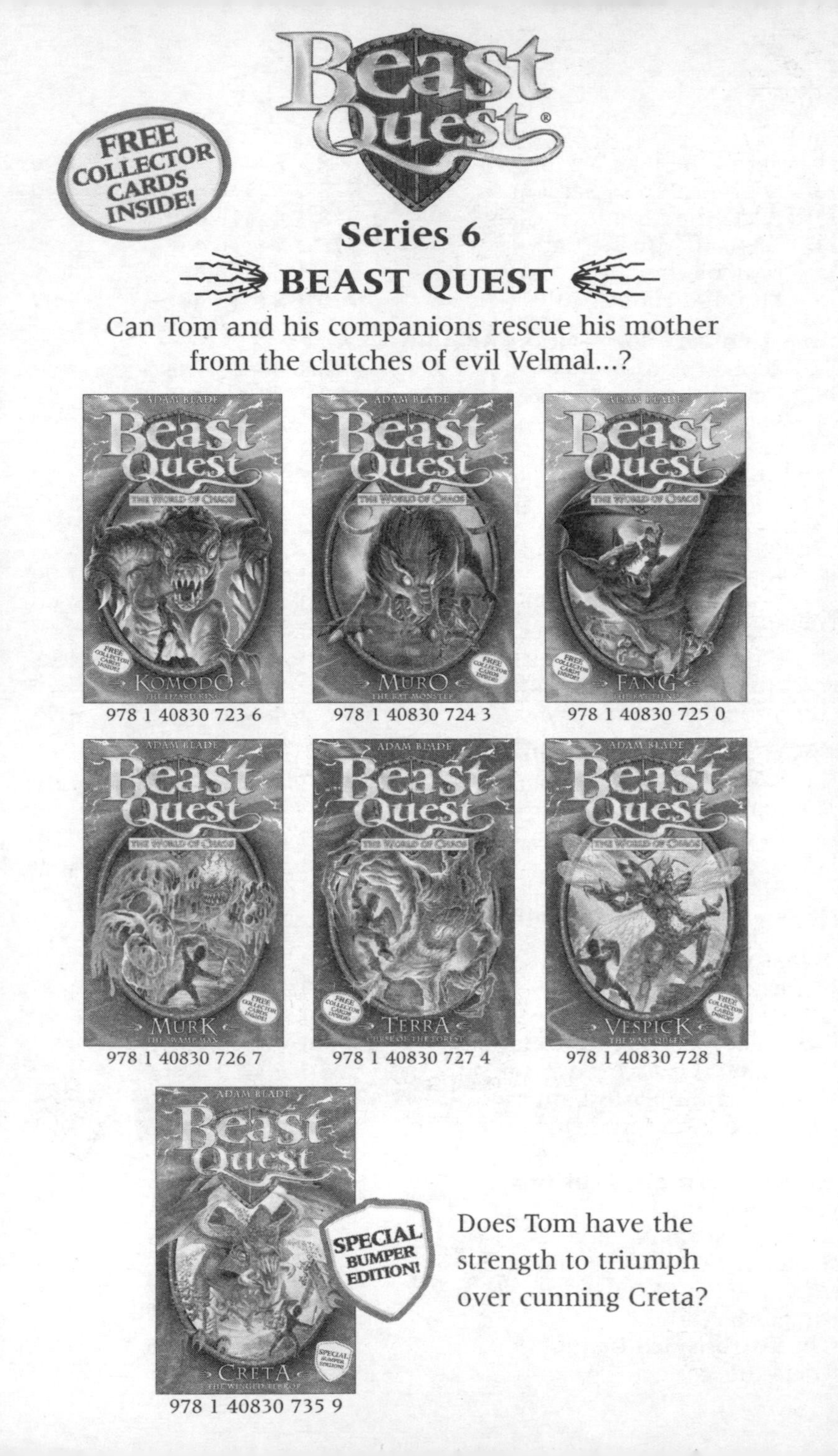
Beast Quest
FREE COLLECTOR CARDS INSIDE!
Series 6
BEAST QUEST
Can Tom and his companions rescue his mother from the clutches of evil Velmal...?
KOMODO
978 1 40830 723 6
MURO
978 1 40830 724 3
FANG
978 1 40830 725 0
MURK
978 1 40830 726 7
TERRA
978 1 40830 727 4
VESPICK
978 1 40830 728 1
CRETA
SPECIAL BUMPER EDITION!
978 1 40830 735 9
Does Tom have the strength to triumph over cunning Creta?

Series 7: THE LOST WORLD

COMING SOON!

978 1 40830 729 8

978 1 40830 730 4

978 1 40830 731 1

978 1 40830 732 8

978 1 40830 733 5

978 1 40830 734 2

The Chronicles of
Avantia

ADAM BLADE
Bestselling author of Beast Quest
The Chronicles of Avantia
FIRST HERO
From the dark, a hero arises
ADAM BLADE, bestselling author of Beast Quest
The Chronicles of Avantia
CHASING EVIL
From the dark, a hero arises
ADAM BLADE, bestselling author of Beast Quest
The Chronicles of Avantia
CALL TO WAR
From the dark, a hero arises
ADAM BLADE, bestselling author of Beast Quest
The Chronicles of Avantia
FIRE AND FURY
From the dark, a hero arises